ALASKAN
VITTLE VERBIAGE!

ALASKAN
VITTLE VERBIAGE!

DJ Blatchford

ReadersMagnet, LLC

Amen Begin

Forgiveness is; The seed of healing.

Healing is; Spontaneous combustion of love.

Love is; The circle of life.

Life is; Through Jesus Christ our Lord.

Amen begin.

ACKNOWLEDGEMENT

This is to really Thank Rain, Florine, and Vince, Gerald and anyone else that helped in bringing my children's book into forishion/furition of today, of Readers Magnet. Here's pointing a finger to you in great gratitude, and humbleness I Quayana (thank you) from the bottom of my heart.

For I have a book of my destiny already and you are apart of it too! So Thank you/Quayaña

My biggest Quayana is to YAH, JC, and Holy Spirit The three biggest loves in and of my life…♡ ♡ ♡

Deuteronomy 1:11 …as he hath promised you, that goes for all of you. YAH bless Israel, as well.

DEDICATION

Here's to acknowledge and dedicate this Children's book Alaskan Vittle Verbiage JLT2! To My Son :Trai-Matthew: I did it with true love and toughs of our times together here on this planet, I know you await me in the Kingdom of our heavenly Father. This book humbly, colorfully expresses my happiness from you and for my time with you, before you graduated to heaven. Your loving kindness will always be a part of my heart. Your joy of berry picking, fishing, hunting, flowers and Ice tea just enjoying life, and always trying to make the best shine forth, I grin when I hear someone say; "You are my sunshine, my only sunshine". So does all the loves of your life, I am sure. You did ask Jesus to come live in your heart, I remember it as it were a day ago! You did a Kárate kick afterwards. Please hug all our family in heaven for us here, Quayana!

So if YAH wills, and we live tomorrow, for it's not promised... if some were left out it was not to be, then again there might just be another book or two!

Amen

Love Mom,

DJ Blatchford

M-m-m-m (Nakuu)= Good, Percy likes his Bear's Steak, Taikuu= Thank you in Inupiat.

Jimbo and Olivia enjoyed Beluga Whale Pizza, Thank you in Inupiaq Quyana, *YAH!*

Trai this hot day is Thankful for Chaga Tea with lemon, Tsin'aen is; Athabacen for Thank you.

Alice Debbie has Buffalo or Bison Burger with Blueberry Shake, Qayaannaqpau is;
Thank you very much in Inupiat.

     DJ BLATCHFORD

Frances serving mush/oatmeal, Danke= Thank you in German.

Kylee asks more milk, please! Thank you in Koniag Alutiiq is; Quyanaa.

Tony's surprise clam chowder snack. Thank you in French= Merci (MEHR-see)

Dingy slips Musk Ox Stew in Unalaska! Thank you in Arabic is; Shukran.

Dawnell snacks on Banic/Fry bread, Sweet and Sour Seal Sandwich.
Thank you in Spanish= Gracias.

Birdsong starts her day with Seagull Boiled Eggs.
Thank you in Italy one says = Grazie.

Mori and Ken munch french fries and American hamburgers with smoothies.
Big thank you in Algonquian-Ojibwe- (Black Feet Indian) is: Chimiigwech.

Micah Oops, grapefruit juice missed his eye. Thank you in Thai= Kop-Khun (cap- coohn)

DJ BLATCHFORD

Jason, serves King Salmon, Sourdocks, and Masu-taters.
Thank you very much in Aluet = Qagaasakuq.

Gloria serves Max, Tom and Cheryl they taste crispy fried bread, rolled in sugar cinnamon called
"walrus flippers", UnangamTunuu (Northern Aluet) ; (Qaguasakung Haqakuq!) means Thank
you all for coming!

M&M dares to share blueberry waffles with *bar-neighbor*. A Mongolian thanks is;
bayarlalaa burkhandaa = YAH/God.

Rykona an Kyona sample Ana'li asdz's (Grandma's) candy Moose nuggets.
Thank you in Cherokee is; Wa do (Wado).

Darren delights in homemade baked Mo-joes-taters with whipped Guacamole dip
by Ajillia-mom. So a Hungarian thank you is; Kos zo nom.

[The o's in word kos zo nom have two dots above the o.]

Patrick and Peaches show happy faces to mom in Mongolian Khan (GenghisKhan) thanks YAH
is; bayarlalaa Burkhandaa. For she made some cherry, cranberry cool whip dessert to eat.

Thank you my good friend in Iroquois Indian is; Nia': wen, as Nathan shows his gratitude by finishing his homemade raspberry jam on sourdough toast.

Nikoia hurrying to finish her much liked homemade wild cranberry waldorf salad. Thank you in Creek Indian is; *Mvto*.

DJ BLATCHFORD

Auntie Rose can hardly wait to dig into the *Grey Whale* barbeque ribs, as her thank you in Filipino is; *Salamat*.

Olivia test fresh blueberry pot pie cobbler, made by Alorah, (*Malo a'upito*) is thank you very much in Tongan.

Sean delights in snacking on an orange, "*Tapadhleat* " is Thank you in *Scottish*.

Jay says hello and thanks in Seneca; Nya: we'h she's for the Beluga Whale roast.

Yummy Deb's Chickweed and wild mushroom quiche, Dixie, Bob and Monica, Mike,
Gott is God Quyanaghhalek tagilusi is thank you for coming *in Siberian Yupik.*

Moe, gets a jester when he pours his cereal, the bag that holds the cereal was not there. Heavenly
(God) Cheers-mate. (Thank you friend, in Australian).

Unk (Uncle) dishes out porcupine lebanon (lasagna), thanks in Greek is; Efcharisto.

Darius delights in hog and hen's eggs for this meal. Thanks in Portuguese is; Brigado,
Holy Spirit (Espirito Santo)! (Brigado Espirito Santo = Thanks Holy Spirit for Comida (food).

 DJ BLATCHFORD

Lily and son Myhi savoured every bite of Bow-head whale burger,
to be thankful (tiazohcamati) to God (Nahuatl) in Aztec.

Kaden awaits his chili reindeer sausage, Qujan is thanks to Anirialuk the Great Spirit; God/YAH.

Slurping dessert Hatchet-Head gives "*meegwetch*" (thank you) to Gitohe Manitou meaning Supreme Being in heaven; God/YAH.

Piper and Gunner hurry scurry for another chocolate chip flapjack and Alaskan birch syrup, Nakelthni =God, Thank you = tsin'aen, my friend (slatsiin), (Ahnta Indian).

     DJ BLATCHFORD

Atius Tirawa = Father Above, Thankfully JJ and Dory nibble on homemade smores,
Hoo = good! (in Pawnee).

Merrily, Mary brings the yummy fried Taters, Go mheanni Dia Duit is May God bless you.
Thank you is Thenk ye in Scottish.

In Brazilian Portuguese; Deus Sega louvodo is "God be praised" for this Alaskan spruce hen crescent sandwich, thank you is Deus obrigado! Exclaims Ashlyn.

Tyler is apparently sharing his deep fried cheese sticks and in Cheyenne thank you is "nease" to Maheo = Creator God, *it's only one mouse!*.

 DJ BLATCHFORD

Mia and this Malimiut = qipmiq is dog, are very grateful for her venison corndog, quyaanaqpak = thank you very much, Ukaktaa = God/the great Iam. *In Inupiaq*

Blackberry, Huckleberry and Blueberry Crepes are a favorite of "Old Crow" means; intelligent with personality an ability, Chuck says Baaiihuli = thank you to, "Manitou" = Great Spirit, in *Crow Indian*.

Mikayla, Jade and Scott impatiently wait to tackle their long awaited tower of sourdough pancakes dripping with homemade Birch Syrup. A stack a woliwon = thank you, to Great Spirit = "Kihci Niweskw" *in Passamaquoddy.*

Sugared cinnamon Alaskan pastry *"Walrus Flipper"* snack to munch on, Marcella likes *Zimbabwe Northern Ndebele* is God bless you, is "alhumdullilah" and I thank you = "Ngiyabonga!".

DJ BLATCHFORD

Jada and a pet mouse in look alike shirts gingerly wait for their serving of much liked macaroni and two cheese delight, Askwali is thank you in *Hopi Indian, Katsina = Great Spirit*.

Chris prays Merci beaucoup = thank you very much and Dieute be'nisse = God bless you. As we consume this way south vittles of oxtail stew. Once enjoyed by the *K'ichai Indians*.

Daniel makes fun blowing bubbles in his Frappe', ashen is thank you to Boha= Super natural Being/God *in Ute – in Shoshone*.

Elder G'ma is tickled to make Isabel grouse and mini dumpling soup *in Croatian* thank you God is; "Hvala Bog"!

   DJ BLATCHFORD

Rebekah snacks on frozen Masu = (wild potatoes) and frozen delicacies keeping in the fresh vitamins Quayanna is thank you *in Inupiaq*, YAH is God in Hebrew.

Popcorn so, hungry for old fashioned slow smoked roasted pigs feet and simmered lima beans with cabbage Mahs = thank you, for this feast = lavasdaa, Nan Gwiltsaii = God *in Gwich'in Indian*.

Thank you is "qugaasakung" to "Agugux" is Creator, Grandma Delice and grandson Liam savor the oven fresh picked Alaskan homemade blueberry pie.

Marie smiles as she prepared a famous Elk and bou/boo (Caribou) gravy on banic fry bread, "style of harmony way" Unetlanvhi = "Great Spirit"!

DJ BLATCHFORD

Randy thoroughly enjoys his clam feast from Clam Gulch, Alaska, Mahalo is thank you,
Mea hana = Creator *in Hawaiian.*

Cuz (Cousin) Chunky displays her half dried an boiled salmon is; Aah nee maak along with
whale blubber = "naniq" *in White Mt. Inupiaq* dialect of Alaska.

Quyana Aunarq= Thank you God *in Inupiaq.*

Tweety enjoys making fresh Duck eggs sunny side up, she states Jesus I Love You = Lesos Konoronhkwa so Thanks a lot is Nia' wenki' wa'hi *in Mohawk Indian*.

Jesse, Bruce, David, Tim and Chief Gary meet for delicious standing Moose= Denaakke' roast with rice, Chin' an gunin =Thank you, you came here, Nakel-thin is God *in Ahtna Indian*.

     DJ BLATCHFORD

Ajillia prepares crab for Family, Thank you very much God! *in Tlingit*,
Gunalche'e shtlien Aanna'awu!

Jared crams Inupiaq Ice cream = "Akutag" or "Kuumanuk" with grandma's hand carved wooly-
mammoth ivory spoon, reward for obeying his master is tupiksriruq in nminik *in Eskimo*,
Quayanna Atanik atanik = Thank you Holy Spirit.

Thank you to all my friends and family good, bad, or indifferent and different, I say Thank you very much. I personally thank my Jesus, God bless Israel, (Deuteronomy 1:11). Please forgive any mistakes in writing, just enjoy, yet thanks again for every & all the hands who helped.

To all the hands that held Monica and still do, thank you and God protect you and Bless You.

Percy enjoys Ham dinner. Quayanna Inupiat (t = *Singular in inupiat*)

In my weakness I am made Strong in YAH's strength. Always being protected by YAH, in some way. He showed me how to bring forth his secrets hidden with in me.

Laughter is a huge beginning of healing. So I endeavor to leave this to you. This is giggles and grins of Characters of some of my family and friends. Remember if you cannot laugh at yourself, be assured others will. (Psalm 46:10-11.) So, as you turn the page may healing be given unto you, may you receive it with YAH's grace and mercies. Many of these characters were a factor in me not giving up in completing this book. Thank you to all your hands of help, (Deuteronomy 1:11), be applied unto you.

Special Thanks to my youngest son Trai, for all our wonderful memories together. He learned the truth just before he left for the kingdom of heaven. He had been told his Mom was a prostitute, when he found out, his Mom was a book author, it gave him peace in his mind and anger to fight against lies told about his Mom. In one of his last talks with me his Mom, he of all of my family said; *"I will help you Mom, I will get two jobs to pay for the advertising of your books you have written, this is how I can help bless you for all the liars and lies told about you, I am so sorry I was misled to believe such things! That meant so much to me and has kept my dreams going when I was led to believe otherwise. Thank you YAH for truth and fighting these battles for me."*

AMEN BEGIN.

DJ Blatchford

[Psalm 46:10-11]

My first Granddaughter Kayla, my miracle grandchild, won beauty contest, at nine. And later was in a near death car wreck. Doctors said she may never walk again and other things on and on. Today with her great attitude, Kayla walked out of the wheelchair, she now runs. Also told she would not have any more children, when her son Noah was just 5 days old.

She has made me a great-Grandma with beautiful great-granddaughter Jada. Kayla inspired me to stay determined not to quit writing my Children's books. Quayanna= thank you my first grandchild love. Thank you for all the prayers and joyful tears of triumph, as she continually gains ground and is still going forward as a great mom, and granddaughter's powerful determination of perfect love of Christ, (John 14:12.)

Thanks to "The Man-Upstairs" (God), Hugo enjoys his southern vittles = food,
his favorite verbiage = language.

Hugo Wesphal sketched his first illustration at the age of three.

He has worked as an artist and illustrator in London, Western Europe and Asia. Skilled in the Tradition of the master realistic works.

Hugo is equally comfortable with pencil, pen and ink, watercolor or oils.

This Dallas artist obviously enjoys bringing smile to the face of a child with his characters.

Quyanna great Grandma sister, :Mary-Apodruq: :Ashenfelter: was lead female Caribou herder, Second in line is Great-grandma :Lena-Apodruk: :Defrane: owner of our goldmine, out of Council, Alaska. Back in the day, of Caribou sleds four travelling. (Why caribou? Run faster than dogs, longer legs.)

DJ BLATCHFORD